TEN OF THE BEST MYTHS,
LEGENDS & FOLK STORIES

TEN OF THE BEST WITCH AND SORCERER STORIES

DAVID WEST

 Crabtree Publishing Company
www.crabtreebooks.com

Crabtree Publishing Company
www.crabtreebooks.com
1-800-387-7650

Publishing in Canada
616 Welland Ave.
St. Catharines, ON
L2M 5V6

Published in the United States
PMB 59051, 350 Fifth Ave.
59th Floor,
New York, NY

Published in **2015 by CRABTREE PUBLISHING COMPANY.**

Printed in the U.S.A./092014/JA20140811

Created and produced by:
David West Children's Books

Project development, design, and concept:
David West Children's Books

Author and designer: David West

Illustrator: David West

Editor: Anastasia Suen

Proofreader: Wendy Scavuzzo

Production coordinator and Prepress technicians:
Samara Parent, Margaret Amy Salter

Print coordinator: Katherine Berti

Photo credits: p8, Walters Art Museum;
p10, Arichis; p12, Bloodofox

Library and Archives Canada Cataloguing in Publication

West, David, 1956-, author
    Ten of the best witch and sorcerer stories / David West.

(Ten of the best : myths, legends & folk stories)
Includes index.
Issued in print and electronic formats.
ISBN 978-0-7787-0797-4 (bound).--ISBN 978-0-7787-1288-6 (pbk.).--
ISBN 978-1-4271-7747-6 (pdf).--ISBN 978-1-4271-7739-1 (pdf)

    1. Tales. I. Title. II. Title: Witch and sorcerer stories.

PZ8.1.W37Wi 2014   j398.21   C2014-903865-8
                                         C2014-903866-6

Library of Congress Cataloging-in-Publication Data

CIP available at Library of Congress

THE STORIES

Circe

*This is the story about an ancient Greek witch and her part in the **Odyssey**.*

Odysseus, king of Ithaca, arrived at the island of Aeaea. Odysseus gave orders for his men to go foraging for food while he stayed with the ship.

Eurylochus, second in command, lead the men inland. After an hour, they saw a column of smoke and headed toward it. Soon they came to a palace surrounded by wild animals that were strangely tame.

From inside the palace came the sound of a woman singing. Eurylochus was scared and hung back but, the rest, led by Polites, entered the palace.

"You are most welcome. Come, there is plenty to eat and drink," said a beautiful woman. It was Circe.

Odysseus was a mythical Greek hero who fought for the Greeks in the Trojan War. He had an epic journey returning home. On one occasion, he escaped rock-throwing giants.

While the Greeks ate their fill, Eurylochus hid outside. Suddenly he heard a screeching sound. Circe had turned the men into wild pigs. Eurylochus fled for his life and warned Odysseus. The hero grabbed his sword and headed for the palace, but he was stopped by the sudden appearance of Hermes, the messenger of the gods. He had been sent by Athena to tell Odysseus to use the herb moly to protect himself from Circe's magic.

When Odysseus arrived at the palace, he drew his sword and demanded Circe release his men from her spell. When the witch's magic didn't work on Odysseus, she gave in and all the animals were returned to their human form.

Circe was said to have been the daughter of Hecate, who was the goddess of magic and witchcraft.

Medea

This story is about a well-known witch of ancient Greece who helped the hero Jason.

One day, a ship arrived on the island of Colchis. The leader of a band of men stepped onto the dock and headed for the palace. His name was Jason. Watching him from her room in the palace was Medea, the daughter of King Aietes of Colchis. She immediately fell in love with Jason.

Jason had come to take the **Golden Fleece**. It was said to be an impossible task since it was guarded by a dragon. But if he succeeded, King Pelias of Iolcus would give up his throne to Jason, who was the rightful heir.

Jason sailed in a ship called the Argo with a band of followers called the Argonauts.

Aietes gave Jason three tasks to perform to win the Golden Fleece. When told of the tasks, Jason knew he could not succeed and fell into a depression. Medea offered to help Jason if he would agree to marry her.

Jason agreed and, with Medea's magic potions, completed the tasks.

Jason and Medea returned to Iolcus where Jason presented the Golden Fleece to Pelias, but the king refused to give up the throne. So Medea used magic to trick the king's two daughters into killing him. The daughters had seen Medea change Jason's ailing father into a younger man and wanted the same for their father. Medea took an old ram and cut it up. She put it in boiling water with magic herbs. When a young ram leaped from the water, the daughters were very excited. They cut up their father and threw the pieces into the pot. But the pieces simply boiled and boiled.

Instead of inheriting the throne, Jason had to flee for his life with Medea because of her witchcraft. They settled in Corinth, where they were married and had two children.

Baba Yaga

This is a tale about how two children escaped the clutches of a Russian witch.

In a vast forest in Russia, twin children came up to a strange house that stood on a giant pair of chicken legs. The evil witch Baba Yaga lived there. The children's cruel stepmother, who was the witch's granddaughter, had sent the twins there to get rid of them.

The witch appeared at the door. "What brings you to Baba Yaga?" she screeched.

"Babushka, we have been sent by our stepmother to live with you," they replied.

"Very well. If you do well enough, I will feed you. If not, I shall eat you up!" Baba Yaga cackled. She immediately set them to work before going into the forest to collect herbs.

The work was very hard and the children began to cry. The mice and birds cried out, "Give us some crumbs and we will help you."

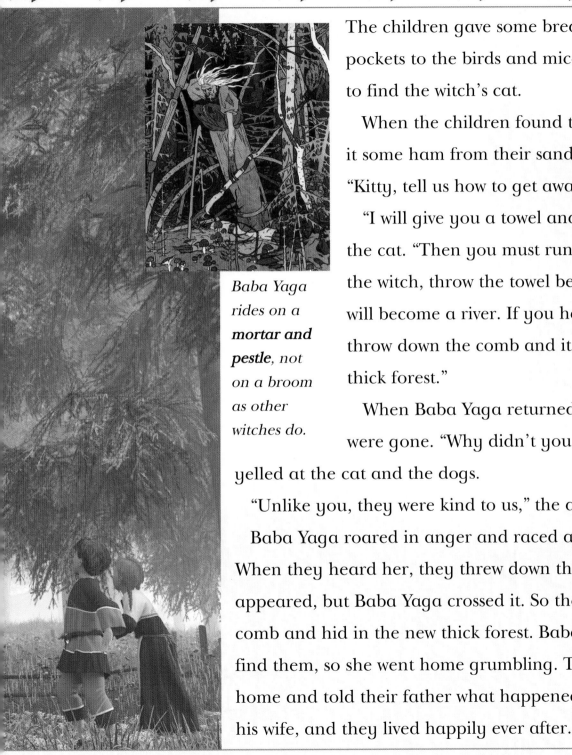

*Baba Yaga rides on a **mortar and pestle**, not on a broom as other witches do.*

The children gave some bread from their pockets to the birds and mice, who told them to find the witch's cat.

When the children found the cat, they gave it some ham from their sandwiches and asked, "Kitty, tell us how to get away."

"I will give you a towel and a comb," said the cat. "Then you must run. When you hear the witch, throw the towel behind you and it will become a river. If you hear her again, throw down the comb and it will become a thick forest."

When Baba Yaga returned, the children were gone. "Why didn't you stop them?" she yelled at the cat and the dogs.

"Unlike you, they were kind to us," the animals replied.

Baba Yaga roared in anger and raced after the children. When they heard her, they threw down the towel. A river appeared, but Baba Yaga crossed it. So they dropped the comb and hid in the new thick forest. Baba Yaga could not find them, so she went home grumbling. The twins ran home and told their father what happened. He threw out his wife, and they lived happily ever after.

The Silver Penny

This folk tale about a kind soldier and a wizard originated in Hungary.

The soldier called Marzi returned after many years in the army to find his parents had died. His brothers had split the inheritance, thinking that he was dead. There was only a silver penny left for him.

The always cheerful Marzi accepted his bad luck and set off on his travels. He came to a wood where he met an old beggar. Marzi gave the old man his silver penny without a second thought. Immediately the old beggar changed into the Wizard of the Wood.

"Your kindness shall be rewarded," the wizard said. "Whatever you wish shall be so."

Marzi replied, "I've always wanted to know what it's like to be an animal."

"Then it shall be so," said the wizard. "Whatever animal you think of, you will become it." Then he disappeared.

Silver pennies first appeared in the eighth century.

A few weeks later, Marzi joined the army of a great king. The king never lost a battle while he wore his ring.

Marching into battle, the king realized he had forgotten his ring.

"Who will fetch my ring and save the day?" the king shouted, but no one answered. It was at least three days' march to the palace. "Whoever succeeds will marry my daughter."

At once, Marzi turned into a hare and set off. A soldier, jealous of Marzi, fired at him but missed. Marzi changed into a salmon to cross rivers, and into a dove to fly over mountains. When he arrived at the palace, he asked the princess for the ring.

Marzi returned with the ring, but the jealous soldier shot him dead. He took the ring and gave it to the king, who then won the battle.

When the army returned to the palace, the princess refused to marry the soldier, telling the king that he was not the right man.

On the battlefield, the Wizard of the Wood found Marzi and brought him back to life. Marzi went back to the palace and the princess pointed him out as the true hero. The jealous soldier was banished from the kingdom and Marzi married the princess.

Mother Hulda

Originally called Frau Holle, this fairy tale from Germany is about a witch with a difference.

There once lived a widow who had a lazy daughter and a beautiful stepdaughter. She made the stepdaughter do all the work and chores around the house, while the daughter was idle and did nothing.

One day, the stepdaughter was sitting by their well spinning when she pricked her finger on the spindle. As she did so, it fell out of her hand and into the well. Knowing that her stepmother would beat her for losing the spindle, she jumped into the water to retrieve it.

Suddenly she found herself in another world, where an old witch called Mother Hulda lived.

"Do not be frightened child," Mother Hulda said. "Come and work for me and I shall look after you."

So the stepdaughter helped Mother Hulda with the chores. She helped bake bread, collected apples from the orchard, and did all the housework without a grumble. After a while, she felt homesick and told Mother Hulda.

"You have worked so well that I will help you go home," said the witch, and she gave her back the spindle she had lost.

She then took the stepdaughter to a gate where a shower of gold fell on her and stuck to her. As she passed through the gate, she magically found herself back near the well at home.

When she explained to her stepmother what had happened, the lazy daughter was sent to do the same. But when she arrived at Mother Hulda's, she was too lazy to help the old witch. When she told the witch that she was homesick, Mother Hulda took her to the gate. But, instead of gold showering upon her, a great kettle of black **pitch** was poured all over her.

So the lazy girl arrived back home covered with pitch—and she could never get it off for as long as she lived.

In Germanic folklore Hulda or Holle was a protector of agriculture and women's crafts such as spinning. She appears either as a crooked-nosed old woman, or as a young maiden clothed in white.

The Witch's Cat

*This German fairy tale is about a kind cat
that helps a witch's captives.*

One summer day, the king's children were playing in the woods when they realized they did not know where they were. Walking along a track was an old woman, so they ran to her and told her they were lost.

"Never mind my dearies," said the old crone. "Come with me and I'll show you how to get home." But instead, she took them back to her house. There she turned into a horrid witch and threw them into a locked room.

The witch had a very clever cat who she thought was under her power, but the cat had fooled her. It had studied her ways and, over time, had learned a lot of magic from her. The cat felt sorry for the children. The next morning, it got up very early and told the bed, "Take my voice and answer for me." It did the same with the stairs and the fireplace. Using magic, it opened the door to the children's room.

"Quick, come," said the cat, and they ran into the forest.

When the witch awoke, she screamed out, "Cat! Get up, you lazy animal, and light the fire!"

The bed answered in the cat's voice, "I will, I will. I'm just washing my whiskers."

A few minutes later, the witch screamed out again. This time, the stairs answered. The next time she screamed, the fire answered. Eventually, the witch became suspicious. When she ran downstairs and discovered the children had escaped with the cat, she screeched with rage, and set off after them. The cat and the children ran, but the witch ran faster. Soon she had almost caught up with them. The cat saw a great stag ahead and yelled out, "These are the king's children! Please help us escape!"

Three hinds carried them on their backs, while the stag captured the witch in his antlers. In the struggle, she lost the ring that gave her all her powers. She was carried off and thrown into a lake, where she drowned. Now that the witch was dead, the cat turned back into its original form—a young girl, who now lives happily with the king's children.

*Witches are often depicted with a cat as their **familiar**.*

Master and Pupil

*This is a Danish fairy story
about a magician and his young servant.*

Once upon a time, there was a magician who employed a young boy to dust his books and keep his home clean. He had asked the boy if he could read. He did not want anyone reading his magic books. The boy lied that he could not read, and he secretly spied on his master and read his magic books.

When he had read all the books, the boy left and returned home. He told his father that he could make money by changing into a horse. His father could sell him to farmers at the fair. The boy would later change back and the farmer would think his horse had run off.

The wizard heard about the horses disappearing and he guessed it was the boy. At the next fair, he bought the horse and took it to have a red hot nail driven into its mouth. This would stop it from changing back into the boy.

The boy became scared and turned into a dove. The magician changed into a hawk to chase the dove. The dove turned into a ring and fell into the lap of a young girl. The hawk changed into a man who offered money for the ring. The ring then became a grain of barley and the man turned into a hen to peck the grain. The grain changed into a **polecat** and bit the hen's head off, killing the wizard. Afterward, the boy married the young girl— and never did magic again.

Books of magic, called grimoires, included instructions on how to perform magic spells.

Hansel and Gretel

*This a famous fairy story from Germany,
collected by the Brothers Grimm.*

Hansel and Gretel lived with their father and their uncaring stepmother. When a great famine settled over the land, she convinced the children's father to abandon them in the woods.

On the first occasion, Hansel left a trail of white pebbles so that they could find their way home at night. The second time, he left a trail of bread crumbs. But the birds ate the crumbs and he and his sister ended up wandering for days. Hungry and lost, they eventually came upon a strange cottage made of cake and gingerbread, and they started to eat it.

An old woman suddenly appeared and asked them in to rest on soft beds. When they awoke, they discovered that the old woman was a wicked witch. She locked Hansel in an iron cage and set Gretel to slave for her. The witch fed Hansel to fatten him up, and after a few weeks, decided it was time to eat him. As she prepared the oven, she asked Gretel to lean in to test the heat. Gretel

suspected the witch wanted to eat her, too, and pretended not to understand. The witch leaned into the oven to show her what she meant. Gretel shoved her in and quickly closed the oven door.

The witch screamed in rage but was burnt to ashes. Gretel ran and released Hansel from the cage. Looking around the house for food, they discovered jewels hidden everywhere. They stuffed their pockets with jewels before setting off to find their home.

After traveling for some time, they came across a wide river.

"How will we get across?" cried Hansel.

"Leave it to me," said Gretel and she called a duckling over. The duckling gave them both a lift across the river. When they arrived home, their father was overjoyed to see them. The stepmother had died and the three of them lived happily ever after on the jewels they had found.

*This tale may have originated during the Great Famine (1315–1317) which caused some people to abandon children and resort to **cannibalism**.*

Aladdin — part one

This is a story of how a wizard tries to trick a simple boy into collecting a magic lamp.

Long ago in ancient Arabia, there lived a wizard who knew of a powerful magic lamp, but it had to be handed to him. So he approached the boy Aladdin in the street and pretended to be his uncle.

Aladdin took him home to meet his mother. The wizard told her that he was the brother of her late husband. "We have never met before as I have been traveling the world," he said. "Now I have returned and am looking for an apprentice to help me. Maybe I could take on your son."

Aladdin's mother was delighted! The wizard bought Aladdin some new clothes and took him into the countryside. After making a small fire, the wizard threw in some powder and uttered a few words. Suddenly, a door appeared in the ground. "Take this torch and bring me the

Originally, this story was set in the Far East and Aladdin was Chinese.

lamp that you will find in the room below, and you shall become rich beyond your wildest dreams," he said, pulling open the door.

Aladdin was fearful but the wizard gave him a magic ring to protect him. He found the lamp and, on the way back, picked from a tree hundreds of gems that were growing. He stuffed the lamp into his jacket so that he could carry the gems. "Help me up!" he shouted to the wizard.

"Give me the lamp first!" cried the wizard. But Aladdin did not want to drop the gems. The wizard thought that Aladdin wanted the lamp for himself! He slammed the door shut and flew back to his home far away.

Aladdin was imprisoned in the dark! "What am I to do?" he wailed, as he rubbed his hands with worry—accidentally rubbing the ring.

Suddenly, a genie appeared. "I am the genie of the ring. What is your command?"

Aladdin wished to be freed, and in an instant he was standing on the hill. He ran home to tell his mother what had happened, and showed her the wizard's lamp.

Aladdin – part two

The evil wizard returns with a plan to get the lamp from Aladdin.

When Aladdin's mother polished the wizard's lamp, the genie of the lamp appeared. Aladdin took the lamp and commanded the genie to bring them food. Soon they wanted for nothing.

Some time later, Aladdin caught sight of the **sultan's** daughter and fell in love. "Mother, I must marry the princess," he said and, remembering the gems he had found, he came up with a plan. He sent his mother with a dish loaded with jewels, to ask for the princess's hand on his behalf.

The greedy sultan was ready to agree but his **vizier** persuaded the sultan to marry the princess to his son instead. Aladdin was not easily put off and used the genies to frighten away the vizier's son, and so ended up marrying the princess himself.

He asked the genies for a palace next door to the sultan's and the couple should have lived happily ever after. But news of Aladdin's success had reached the wizard, who wanted to get the lamp from him.

Genies, or jinns, are supernatural creatures in ancient Arabian mythology. They live in another dimension from ours but can appear and interact in our world to do good or evil.

When Aladdin was away, the wizard appeared outside the palace giving new lamps for old. People laughed at him but, the princess, who knew nothing of the powers of Aladdin's lamp, gave it to the wizard in exchange for a new one. Immediately, the wizard summoned the genie and had the palace and the princess taken to his own home far away.

When Aladdin returned and discovered what had happened, he summoned the genie of the ring to take him to his palace. Aladdin found the princess and gave her some poison to put in the wizard's drink. When the wizard was dead, he commanded the genie of the lamp to take them back home—and this time, they did end up living happily ever after.

GLOSSARY

cannibalism The practice of humans eating the flesh of other human beings

familiar A demon under the spell of a witch, often said to take the form of an animal

Golden Fleece The woolly coat of the gold-haired, winged ram, which was a symbol of authority and kingship

mortar and pestle A small bowl and crushing tool, used for grinding herbs

Odyssey The story of Odysseus's journey

pitch An old name for sticky, black substances such as tar and asphalt, or bitumen

polecat The common name for weasel-like Eurasian mammals that hunt small mammals

sultan Middle Eastern ruler

vizier A high-ranking political adviser to a ruler

INDEX